# A Bumblebee Sweater

To Molly Frost
*—Betty*

For Louise
*—Kim*

Text copyright © 2008 by Betty Waterton

Illustrations copyright © 2008 by Kim LaFave

Published in Canada by Fitzhenry & Whiteside,
195 Allstate Parkway, Markham, Ontario L3R 4T8

Published in the United States by Fitzhenry & Whiteside,
311 Washington Street, Brighton, Massachusetts 02135

www.fitzhenry.ca   godwit@fitzhenry.ca

10 9 8 7 6 5 4 3 2 1
**Library and Archives Canada Cataloguing in Publication**
Waterton, Betty, 1923-
A bumblebee sweater / Betty Waterton ; illustrated by Kim LaFave.
ISBN-13: 978-1-55455-028-9 (bound)        ISBN-10: 1-55455-028-9 (bound)
I. LaFave, Kim  II. Title.
PS8595.A796B86 2008        jC813'.54        C2006-906874-7

**U.S. Publisher Cataloging-in-Publication Data
(Library of Congress Standards)**

Waterton, Betty.
A bumblebee sweater / Betty Waterton; illustrated by Kim LaFave
[32] p.: col. ill.;  cm.
Summary: Grandma knits a new sweater for Nellie's role as a bumblebee in the upcoming
concert, but every time she wears the sweater, Nellie gets into a scrape.
ISBN-10: 1-55455-028-9        ISBN-13:  978-1-55455-028-9
1. Grandmothers —Fiction – Juvenile literature.  I. LaFave, Kim.  II. Title.
[E]  dc22  PZ7 .W384  2008

Fitzhenry & Whiteside acknowledges with thanks the Canada Council for the Arts, and the
Ontario Arts Council for their support of our publishing program. We acknowledge the
financial support of the Government of Canada through the Book Publishing Industry
Development Program (BPIDP) for our publishing activities.

Design by Wycliffe Smith Design Inc.

Printed in Hong Kong, China

# A Bumblebee Sweater

by Betty Waterton

Illustrated by Kim LaFave

Fitzhenry & Whiteside

One wintry day, Grandma Needlethorpe
got a letter in
the mail.

Inside was a picture drawn by little Nellie.
And underneath it was a note.

Squinting, Grandma Needlethorpe held up the picture close to her eyes.

"It's BEE-YEW-TIFUL!" she exclaimed. "I must make Nellie a sweater to wear in the concert."

So Grandma Needlethorpe searched for her spectacles.

Then she hunted for her knitting needles.

Finally she rooted around for the right colors of wool.

One spring day, Nellie got a parcel in the mail.

"I see it's come from Grandma," said Nellie's mom. "But whatever can it be? It's such a funny shape. It looks like a *T*."

"That's a sweater shape," said Nellie. "See? It's got two arms."

"And an awful lot of sticky tape," said Dad.

So they peeled and they
peeled and they peeled, and
at last they got the sticky
tape off the parcel.

Then they peeled and they peeled, and they got the sticky tape off Nellie.

Then they peeled the tape off Sparky.

And when they opened the parcel, there was a beautiful sweater, knit by Grandma Needlethorpe herself.

"Wow, it's BEE-YEW-TIFUL!" cried Nellie, pulling the sweater over her head. "Now I can be the bumblebee for sure."

"A rather large bumblebee," said Mom. "This sweater is WAY too big." And she turned back the sleeves.

"That's all right," said Nellie. "I like it big. It'll keep my knees warm."

The next day, Nellie put on her new sweater.

"I just want to show it to my friends at school," she said.

"Just be sure to keep it nice for the concert," said Mom.

"Oh, Nellie, it's BEE-YEW-TIFUL!" said her friends.

But at lunchtime, Nellie had a little spill.

"Oops," said Nellie, and she turned the sweater around.

When Mrs. Needlethorpe saw Nellie's back, she sighed. Then straightaway she put the sweater into the wash.

The next day, Nellie wore her new sweater again.

"Just because it's a little cold and rainy," she said.

"I'll be careful."

But when she ran out to the baseball field, she had a little tumble.

"Oops," said Nellie, and she turned the sweater around.

Then, during the game, Nellie took a little slide.

"Oops," said Nellie, and she turned the sweater around again.

When Mrs. Needlethorpe saw Nellie's front and back, she groaned. Then straightaway she put the sweater into the wash.

The next day, Nellie wore her new sweater again. "Because I want to look special for Cousin Stephanie's party," she said. "I promise I'll be REALLY careful."

But at the party, she had a cherry cream soda.
"Oops," said Nellie, and she turned the sweater around.
Then there was cake and ice cream.
"Oops," said Nellie, and she turned the sweater around again.

But then they played tag with jelly bears and tossed balloons, and Nellie was having too much fun to turn her sweater around.

Straightaway Mrs. Needlethorpe threw the sweater
into the wash, muttering grimly to herself.

The day before the concert, Nellie put on her sweater again.

"We're going on an educational trip. On the bus. I can't get messy this time."

The Duck Farm *was* educational. But Nellie's sweater got a little messy again. Well, REALLY messy. With quite a lot of duck doo.

"Phew!" said Mrs. Needlethorpe, and straightaway she put the sweater in a special wash, all by itself.

But this time, when the sweater came out of the dryer, she cried, "Yikes! It really shrank this time. Now what will Nellie wear to the concert?"

When Nellie came home from school the next day, she said, "Guess what? I'm not going to be a bumblebee after all! We got our costumes today, and I'm going to be a flower with the other girls!"

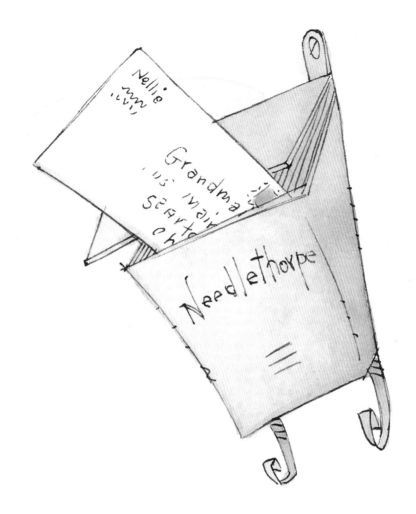

One summery day, Grandma Needlethorpe got
an envelope in the mail. Inside was a beautiful
photograph. Squinting, Grandma Needlethorpe
held up the picture close to her eyes.

"There's the sweater I sent Nellie," she said. "It fits her quite well, I see. But…" Grandma Needlethorpe squinted again.

"Just look at those other children in her class.
My, they're really HUGE beside our Nellie."